This book belongs to:

_____

Contents

Ladybird

Cover illustration by Guy Parker-Rees

Published by Ladybird Books Ltd
27 Wrights Lane London W8 5TZ
A Penguin Company

2 4 6 8 10 9 7 5 3 1

© LADYBIRD BOOKS LTD MCMXCVII, MMI

Printed in Italy

My secret book of rules

written by Geraldine Taylor
illustrated by Guy Parker-Rees

Rules for my mum

Give me chocolate ice cream
six times a day and
let me keep my worm collection
in my bedroom and
let me keep my smelly socks on
all night — they're nice and warm.

Don't tell me to kiss my little sister
and don't look at me when
my dad falls on a marble...

I didn't put it there!

5

Rules for my dad

Don't tell me to be nice
to my little sister and
then blame me when she gets
all messy.
I am being nice to her.

Don't make me put my worms back
in the garden and don't yell,
"Keep that horrible dog away
from me!" when my dog runs in
the mud and smells.

I can't help it!

Rules for my little sister

Stop getting me into trouble
with my dad.

Why can't you tell him we **are**
playing nicely?

Stop smelling and please stop
yelling — my ears don't like it.

Hurry up and get big enough
to play football and say
"thank you" when I put worms
in your T-shirt.

Rules for my teacher

Put a big red star next to
all my spellings and
put a big gold star on
all my maths and tell my mum
I'm amazingly brilliant and
don't yell, "Did you bring that horrible
mouse to school again?"
when my mouse gets out of
my pocket and runs about.

It's not my fault!

$$9 + 3 = 11$$

Rules for my dog

Don't sit under my chair when I'm eating my dinner and make smells. Everyone looks at me and says "Stop it!" and **it's not fair!**

Don't keep putting your wet nose in my pocket – my mouse doesn't like it.

Don't dig up Dad's best rose trees. I don't need you to help me find my worms.

Don't lick my knees.
It's horrible.
Go and lick my sister.

Rules for my mouse

Come when I call you and don't go round the back of the washing machine and stay there all night and don't wriggle about in my pocket and don't jump out and run around when my teacher's looking and please, please, please keep away from my mum.

You can play with my little sister.

Rules for EVERYONE EVERYWHERE

Be nice to me and my dog and my mouse.

Don't look at me when there's a smell in the room.

Don't give me horrible kisses. Give them to my little sister.

Don't pull a cross face when I show you my worm collection.

And when something horrible happens...

Peaches

19p

17

DON'T BLAME ME!

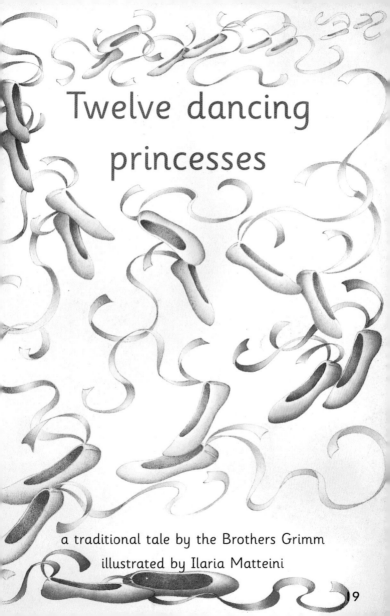

Twelve dancing princesses

a traditional tale by the Brothers Grimm

illustrated by Ilaria Matteini

Once there was a king who had twelve beautiful daughters.
They all slept in the same room, and every night the King made sure that they were safely locked in.

But every morning the princesses were tired and their shoes were all worn through.

"What do my daughters do each night?" asked the King. But no one knew.

At last the King announced that anyone who could solve the mystery could marry one of the princesses.

Many princes tried, but not one could keep awake long enough to see.

One day a soldier made his way to the palace. An old woman met him and said, "The princesses are under a magic spell. Don't drink anything they bring you.
Just pretend to fall asleep."
Then she gave him a cloak.
"This will make you invisible when you follow the princesses."

That night, at the palace,
the eldest princess gave the soldier
some wine. He pretended to drink
it and then lay down as if he were
asleep.

At once the princesses got up and
dressed in their finest clothes
and jewels. Then they opened
the door to a magic stairway.
The soldier quickly put on his
magic cloak and followed
the princesses.

First they came to an enchanted
woodland. The soldier broke off
three shining branches and put them
under his cloak.
"I'll show these to the King,"
he thought.

Then the princesses came to
a magnificent palace.
They danced there until
three o'clock in the morning.
At last they went home with their
shoes quite worn through.

The soldier hurried back too.

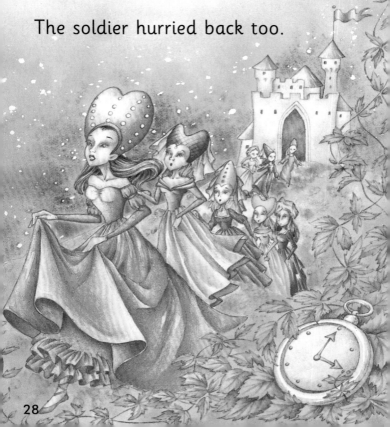

The next morning he showed
the King the three shining branches,
and told him everything
that had happened.

The King sent for his daughters and asked them if the soldier was telling the truth.

"Yes," they said sadly.

The princesses were sorry now that they had deceived their father.

The soldier married the eldest princess, and they all lived happily ever after.

The meeting

adapted from a poem by Derek Dwyer
illustrated by David Parkins

He was standing in our garden,
Looked at me and asked my name.
Told me once he used to live here,
But it didn't look the same.

He was glad we'd kept the apple tree.
He was happy now he'd been.
Said that I could tell my mum
I'd met a man called Sammy Green.

When I told my mum, her face went
    white;
She didn't say a lot.
I didn't ask her what was wrong,
I thought I'd better not.

But when I was in the graveyard,
I think I found out why.
I found the grave of Sammy Green...
And an apple tree nearby.